Dear Parent:
Your child's love of reading starts here!

Every child learns to read in a different way and at his or her own speed. Some go back and forth between reading levels and read favorite books again and again. Others read through each level in order. You can help your young reader improve and become more confident by encouraging his or her own interests and abilities. From books your child reads with you to the first books he or she reads alone, there are I Can Read Books for every stage of reading:

SHARED READING
Basic language, word repetition, and whimsical illustrations, ideal for sharing with your emergent reader

BEGINNING READING
Short sentences, familiar words, and simple concepts for children eager to read on their own

READING WITH HELP
Engaging stories, longer sentences, and language play for developing readers

READING ALONE
Complex plots, challenging vocabulary, and high-interest topics for the independent reader

ADVANCED READING
Short paragraphs, chapters, and exciting themes for the perfect bridge to chapter books

I Can Read Books have introduced children to the joy of reading since 1957. Featuring award-winning authors and illustrators and a fabulous cast of beloved characters, I Can Read Books set the standard for beginning readers.

A lifetime of discovery begins with the magical words "I Can Read!"

Visit www.icanread.com for information
on enriching your child's reading experience.

For Daniel William and Adam Joshua,
brothers and best friends!
—A.S.C.

HarperCollins®, ☙®, and I Can Read Book® are trademarks of HarperCollins Publishers.

Library of Congress Cataloging-in-Publication Data
Capucilli, Alyssa Satin, date.
  Biscuit's day at the farm / story by Alyssa Satin Capucilli ; pictures by Pat Schories.—1st ed.
    p.   cm.—(My first I can read)
  Summary: Biscuit the dog meets hens, pigs, geese, and goats while visiting a farm.
ISBN 978-0-06-074167-9 (trade bdg.) — ISBN 978-0-06-074168-6 (lib. bdg.) — ISBN 978-0-06-074169-3 (pbk.)
  [1. Dogs—Fiction. 2. Farms—Fiction. 3. Domestic animals—Fiction.] I. Schories, Pat, ill. II. Title. III. Series: My first I can read book.
PZ7.C179Bitm 2006   2006000562
[E]—dc22   CIP
                                                                                                                              AC

❖

11 12 13 LP/WOR 10 9 8 7 6

Biscuit's Day at the Farm

story by ALYSSA SATIN CAPUCILLI
pictures by PAT SCHORIES

HarperCollins*Publishers*

Come along, Biscuit.
We're going to help
on the farm today.

Woof, woof!

We can feed the hens, Biscuit.

Woof, woof!

We can feed the pigs, too.

The pigpen
is empty, Biscuit.
Where can the pigs be?

Woof, woof!

Funny puppy.

You found the pig
and the piglets, too.
Woof!

Let's feed the goats,
Biscuit.
Woof, woof!

Oink!

Oh, Biscuit.

The piglet is out of the pen.

We must put
the piglet back.
Woof, woof!

Let's feed the sheep, Biscuit.

Woof, woof!

Oink!

Oh no, Biscuit.

It's the piglet!

We must put the piglet back
one more time.

Woof, woof!

Here are the geese,
Biscuit.

Woof, woof!

Oink!

Here is the piglet again.

Woof, woof!

Oink! Oink!

Honk!

Wait, Biscuit!
The geese are just
saying hello.

Woof!

Silly puppy!
The piglet is back
in the pen.

And so are you, Biscuit!

Oink!

Woof, woof!